YOUR Life MATTERS

CHRIS SINGLETON

ILLUSTRATED BY
TAYLOR BARRON

Headlines glow.
Sirens wail.
A question presses
in the dark:

DOES MY LIFE
MATTER?

Heads turn.
Eyes shift.
The world's an
invisible place.

DOES MY LIFE
MATTER?

Doors slam.
Ground slides.
The future seems
to dim.

DOES MY LIFE
MATTER?

Oh child, your life matters more than you can possibly ever know. From the tips of your hair to the lengths of your toes, you are beautifully and wonderfully made.

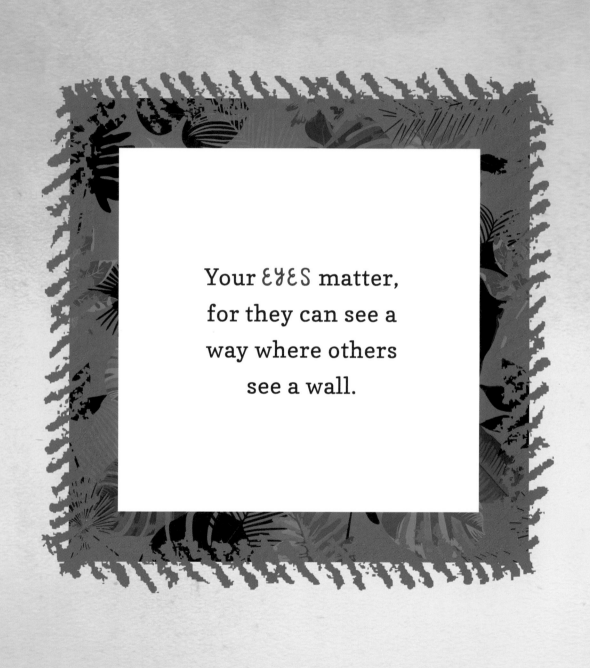

Your EYES matter,
for they can see a
way where others
see a wall.

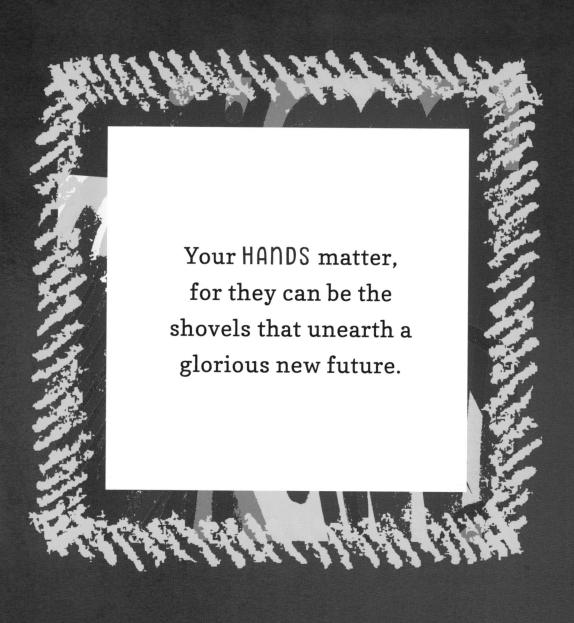

Your HANDS matter,
for they can be the
shovels that unearth a
glorious new future.

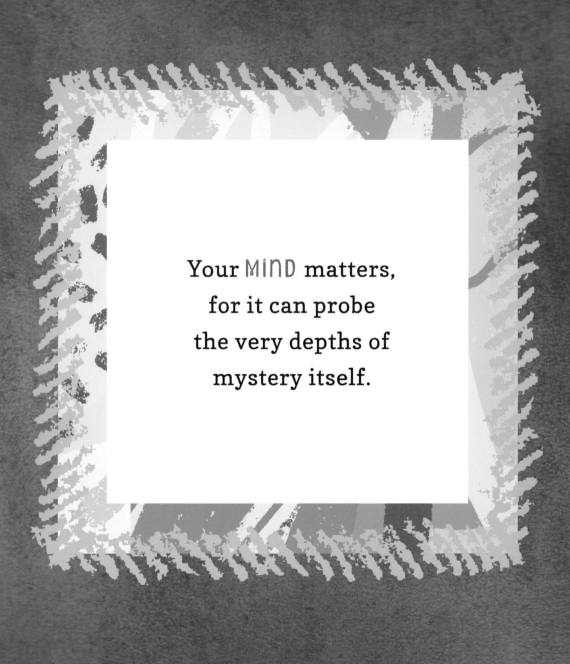

Your MIND matters,
for it can probe
the very depths of
mystery itself.

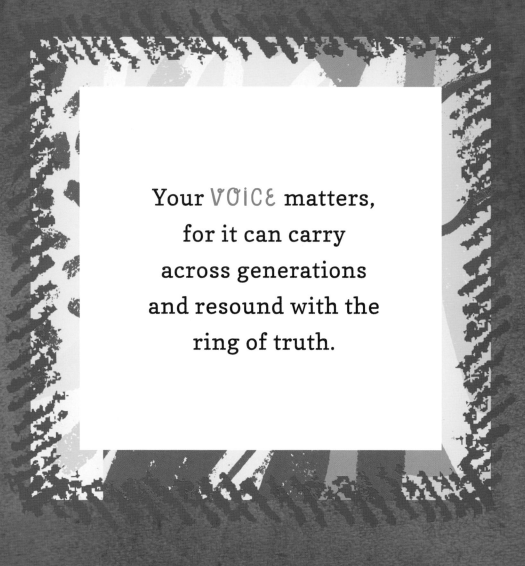

Your VOICE matters,
for it can carry
across generations
and resound with the
ring of truth.

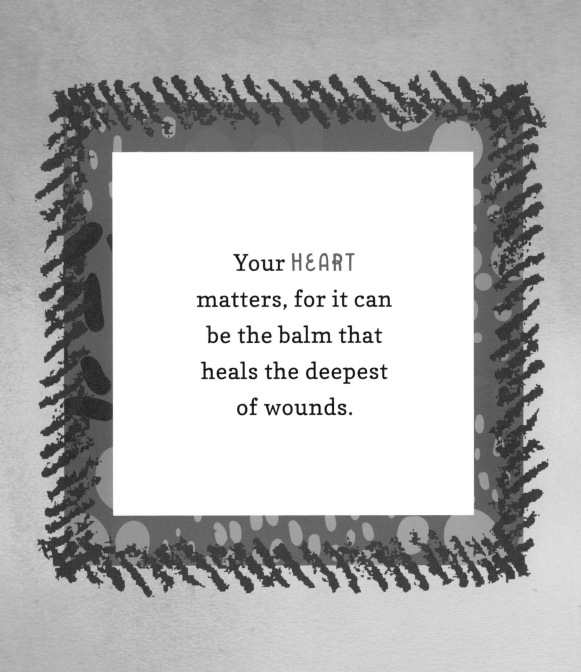

Your HEART matters, for it can be the balm that heals the deepest of wounds.

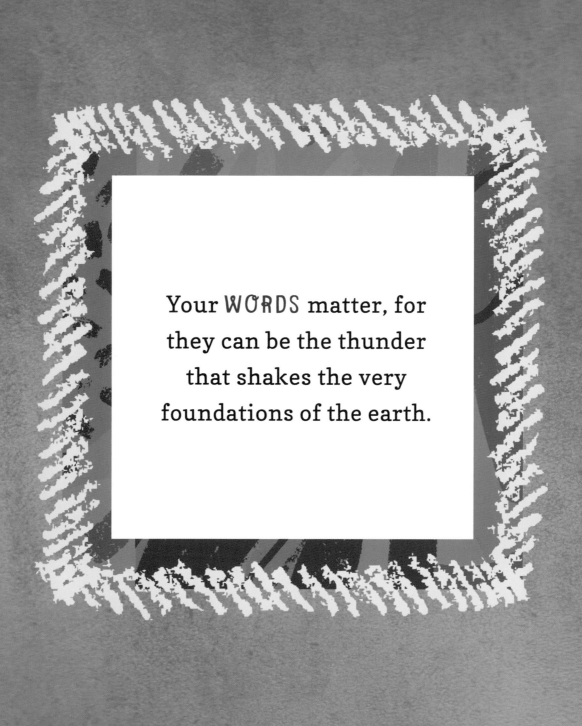

Your WORDS matter, for they can be the thunder that shakes the very foundations of the earth.

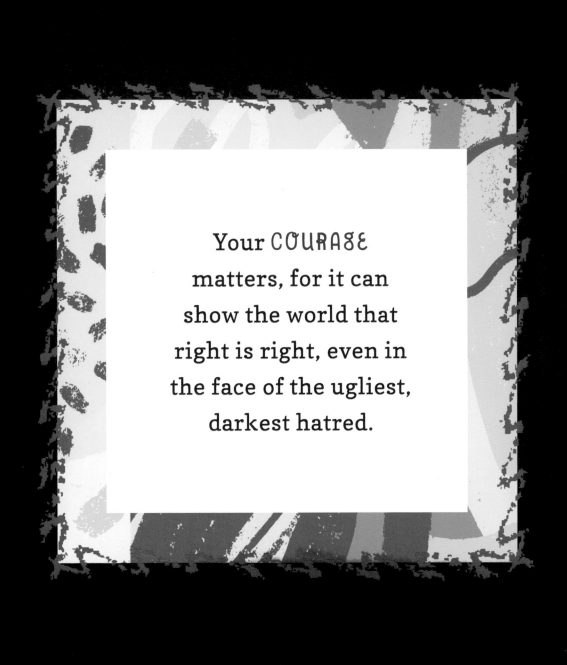

Your COURAGE
matters, for it can
show the world that
right is right, even in
the face of the ugliest,
darkest hatred.

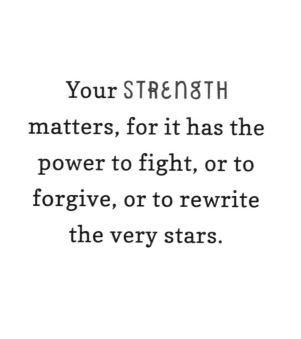

Your STRENGTH matters, for it has the power to fight, or to forgive, or to rewrite the very stars.

So rewrite those stars, child. Sketch your dreams high in the heavens. We are with you. And when the world feels upside down, we will remind you again and again . . .

MEET THE HEROES ROOTING FOR YOU

HARRIET TUBMAN (1822–1913)

Nicknamed "Grandma Moses," Harriet helped around seventy slaves escape to freedom. Despite facing low odds and everpresent danger, her record was incredible: not a single escaped slave in her charge was lost in his or her flight to freedom.

BARACK OBAMA (1961–)

Barack was elected the first Black president of the United States. Prior to his service in government, he worked as a community organizer in Chicago where he fought to improve job training and housing.

KATHERINE JOHNSON (1918–2020)

Katherine graduated from high school by age fourteen and from college by age eighteen. Her remarkable math skills led to a job at NASA where she helped calculate the trajectory for Alan Shephard's space flight (the first American in space) and for the Apollo 11 flight to the moon.

GEORGE WASHINGTON CARVER (1860s–1943)

The most famous Black scientist in the early 1900s, George developed new ways to farm that would protect nutrients in the soil and give farmers a better crop. He also pioneered innovative uses for the peanut, sweet potato, and other plant foods. A lab, a museum, and even a submarine have been named in his honor.

MARTIN LUTHER KING, JR. (1929–1968)

Martin helped lead the civil rights movement that eventually brought about the Civil Rights Act of 1964. He used his voice to preach freedom and taught others that nonviolent activism could bring about change. Sadly, Martin was assassinated when he was just thirty-nine years old.

OPRAH WINFREY (1954–)

When Oprah was a girl, her family was so poor that she sometimes had to wear dresses made from potato sacks. After winning a speech contest, she was given a scholarship to college and eventually rose to become one of the most famous talk-show hosts in history. Oprah is known for her kindness and generosity.

MAYA ANGELOU (1928–2014)

Maya used her gift with the pen to speak out on racism and teach about identity and family. Her poems and autobiographies are read all over the world. At President Bill Clinton's inauguration, she delivered her most famous poem yet—"On the Pulse of the Morning"—and encouraged listeners to fight for a better future.

JACKIE ROBINSON (1919–1972)

As the first Black player for a Major League Baseball team, Jackie faced tremendous opposition and ridicule from people who thought Black people didn't belong. But Jackie's courage, skill, and determination to not fight back won much of the country over.

MUHAMMAD ALI (1942–2016)

Considered one of the greatest boxers of all time, Muhammad was as kind out of the ring as he was fierce in it. He is said to have never refused an autograph and was known to give generously to many causes. One sports magazine named him the greatest athlete of the 20th century.

TEGLA LOROUPE (1973–)

In 1998, Tegla became the first African woman to hold the world record for the fastest-run marathon. She used her influence to create Peace Marathons where members of different tribes in her native Kenya run together to promote peace instead of tribal fighting.

DEDICATED TO THE MEMORY OF SHARONDA
COLEMAN-SINGLETON, CHRISTOPHER ROBIN
SINGLETON, AND THE VICTIMS OF THE
MOTHER EMANUEL 9. — C. S.

TO ALL OF THE ACTIVISTS AROUND THE
WORLD FOR CONTINUING TO FIGHT FOR
REAL CHANGE. YOUR EMPATHY AND
STRENGTH ARE BEAUTIFUL! — T. B.

BUSHEL & PECK BOOKS

Text copyright © 2020 by Chris Singleton and David Miles.
Illustration copyright © 2020 by Taylor Barron.

Published by Bushel & Peck Books, a family-run publishing house in Fresno, California, who
believes in uplifting children with the highest standards of art, music, literature, and ideas. Find
books, gifts, and more for gifted young minds at www.bushelandpeckbooks.com.

Type set in Copse, Chelsea Market Pro, and Undersong Solid.

Bushel & Peck Books is dedicated to fighting illiteracy all over the world. For every book we sell,
we donate one to a child in need—book for book. To nominate a school or organization to receive
free books, please visit www.bushelandpeckbooks.com.

Crayon doodle design elements and textured backgrounds licensed from Shutterstock.com.

LCCN: 2020948427
ISBN: 9781952239311

First Edition

Printed in China

10 9 8 7 6 5 4 3 2 1